For Renaud and Béatrice

Library of Congress Cataloging-in-Publication Data

Dupasquier, Philippe.
  The great escape.

  Originally published: England: Walker Books, 1988.
  Summary: In this story without words, an escaped
prisoner leads the police on an exciting chase.
  [1. Escapes—Fiction.   2. Prisoners—Fiction.
3. Stories without words]   I. Title.
PZ7.D924Gr 1988   [Fic]   87-21500
ISBN 0-395-46806-X

Copyright © 1988 by Philippe Dupasquier
Published in the United States by Houghton Mifflin Company
Published in England by Walker Books

Printed and bound by L.E.G.O., Vicenza, Italy

10 9 8 7 6 5 4 3 2 1

THE GREAT ESCAPE

PHILIPPE DUPASQUIER

Houghton Mifflin Company
Boston 1988

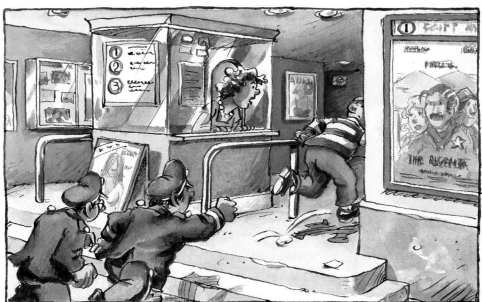

THE END...